Geek alert

"Good morning, class," said Mrs. Wooden cheerfully. "We have a new student with us today. His name is Sean O'Malley, and he's just arrived in Washington, D.C., from New Jersey."

Joshua had to crane his neck to see the new boy.

"Looks more like he arrived from midget land," someone whispered. The class laughed, and Mrs. Wooden had to clap her hands for silence.

She told the new boy to take the empty seat in the back.

"Right next to Joshua Bates," she said. The new boy walked quietly to his seat.

"Joshua," Mrs. Wooden announced, "seeing as Sean is new to Mirch Elementary, I think it would be nice if you showed him around."

Joshua groaned.

"What did you say, Joshua?"

"Yes, Mrs. Wooden."

"That's better."

A Knopf Paperback by the same author:

The Flunking of Joshua T. Bates

Joshua T. Bates
Takes Charge

Susan Shreve

illustrated by
Dan Andreasen

A KNOPF PAPERBACK
Alfred A. Knopf · New York

A KNOPF PAPERBACK BOOK PUBLISHED BY ALFRED A. KNOPF, INC.

http://www.randomhouse.com/

Library of Congress Cataloging-in-Publication Data
Shreve, Susan Richards.
Joshua T. Bates takes charge / by Susan Shreve ; illustrated by Dan Andreasen.
p.   cm.
Summary: Eleven-year-old Joshua, worried about fitting in at school, feels awkward
when the new student he is supposed to be helping becomes the target of the fifth
grade's biggest bully. Sequel to "The Flunking of Joshua T. Bates."
[1. Schools — Fiction. 2. Popularity — Fiction. 3. Bullies — Fiction.]
I. Title.
PZ7.S55915Jo   1993   [Fic] — dc20   92-19708
ISBN 0-679-87039-3 (pbk.)

First Knopf Paperback edition: October 1997
Printed in the United States of America
10 9 8 7 6 5 4 3 2

TO

Abbai B., Adam F., Adam M., Adam W., Alex C.,
Andrew F., Caleb S., Chris B., Chris M., Chris Z.,
Colin M., David D., Francis F., Hamet W., Jim S.,
Kwame V., Liam G., Neal T., Paul T., Ryan G.,
and Sheeraz H.

AND TO

Kate McKay, whom they will always love

Joshua T. Bates
Takes Charge

chapter one

JOSHUA T. BATES was just beginning to recover from the worst year of his life. Even now, whenever he walked down the corridor to the library or up the steps to the gym or out to the playground, he was certain at least some of the children at Mirch Elementary were whispering, "That's Joshua Bates. Remember? He's the one who flunked third grade."

"Children forget what happened last year, darling," his mother had told him. "And besides, you were promoted."

"You're wrong about children," Joshua said. "They always remember the bad things about you."

The bad thing that happened to Joshua was that at the end of third grade his parents were told by his teacher that he would have to repeat third grade. Which is exactly what happened that September when he should have been in the

3

fourth grade. All that fall of his second year in third grade Joshua worked harder than he had ever worked in his life, and in November, after Thanksgiving, he was promoted to the fourth grade.

Now Joshua had trouble sleeping. He worried about Miss Lacey's fifth-grade math class, in which he was getting a D. He worried about baseball and whether he'd get to play pitcher this spring. He worried about the five dollars that he'd gotten from his grandmother for his birthday and lost when he was wearing his blue jeans with the hole in the pocket. But mostly he worried about being left out.

In the fifth grade at Mirch Elementary the only possible way to be included as a regular boy was for Tommy Wilhelm to like you. The fact was, Tommy Wilhelm and Joshua not only were *not* friends, they were true enemies, and had been ever since Tommy pushed Joshua down the school steps in first grade and no one told the teacher, not even Joshua.

Joshua was not exactly afraid of Tommy, but he was careful.

It was the first day of school after holiday vacation, and already things had started badly for Joshua. He arrived at school bad-tempered. First off, for Christmas he got chickenpox, which meant that he couldn't go skiing. Instead he had to stay at home with his mother and two-year-old sister Georgianna while his father had taken Amanda, his brainy older sister, skiing. As far as Joshua could tell, Amanda didn't even know how to do anything except read books and talk on the telephone.

And then this morning Georgianna spilled her applesauce on the new ski sweater Joshua had gotten for Christmas but hadn't yet been able to wear because he couldn't go skiing and had to spend most of his time in bed or on the couch watching TV, and as a result of having to wash off the applesauce he arrived at school late. Running up the steps of Mirch Elementary and right in front of Tommy Wilhelm and Billy Nickel, he fell, ripping one knee of his blue jeans and cutting his shin so that blood trickled down his leg.

"Smooth move, Princess," Billy said. He and Tommy laughed.

"Yeah, Josh," Tommy chipped in, "you okay? Do you need a nurse?"

"Maybe he needs his mommy!" Billy said.

"Yeah!" Tommy agreed.

"Joshua needs his mommy! Joshua needs his mommy!" Tommy and Billy chanted. They burst out laughing.

Billy walked up to Joshua.

"What's happened to your face, Joshua?" Billy asked. "You got zits like my sister and you're only eleven."

"Chickenpox, lamebrain," Joshua said. "Ever hear of chickenpox?"

"Yeah, I heard of chickenpox." Billy smirked. "But I had them in third grade, which means you must have had them twice!"

"Good one, Billy!" Tommy roared. Billy grinned, and they exchanged high-fives.

Joshua felt like punching them both right on the nose. Instead he climbed the rest of the stairs, passed through the big double doors of Mirch Elementary, limped down the hall, and took his regular seat in Mrs. Wooden's fifth-grade class.

TOMMY WILHELM was the chief commander of the fifth grade. He had short black curly hair and was built like a dump truck. He had a square face and bright pink cheeks. He was, hands down, the most powerful boy in the fifth grade, maybe in all of Mirch Elementary, as far as Joshua could tell. And he always had been, ever since first grade, when he arrived from Dallas, Texas, and immediately began beating up the smaller boys behind the equipment shed and pulling down the girls' pants on the lower game field. Worst of all, Tommy hardly ever got in trouble. Even, for example, when he rubbed spit into Sally Loehr's hair or pushed Adam Speth's head into the toilet after gym class, no one told. All the students were afraid of him.

Billy Nickel was his sidekick. What Tommy Wilhelm wanted done, Billy Nickel would do.

When Joshua flunked third grade, Tommy teased him practically every day and even threatened to beat up any fourth grader who talked to Joshua or played with him, including Andrew Porter, Joshua's best friend.

Tommy and Joshua got into a fight.

"You killed him!" Billy Nickel had shouted.

"Not yet," Joshua had said.

Tommy Wilhelm had cried, and had even promised to stop teasing Joshua.

"Okay," Joshua had said.

But it wasn't okay. In fact, it wasn't okay at all.

"GOOD MORNING, CLASS," said Mrs. Wooden cheerfully. "And happy New Year."

"Good morning and happy New Year," the children mumbled. Joshua rubbed his shin, which hurt, but the bleeding seemed to have stopped.

"Children, we have a new student with us today. His name is Sean O'Malley, and he's just arrived in Washington, D.C., from New Jersey."

Joshua had to crane his neck to see the new boy.

"Looks more like he arrived from midget land," someone whispered. Probably Tommy Wilhelm, Joshua thought. The class laughed, and Mrs. Wooden had to clap her hands for silence.

She told the new boy to take the empty seat in the back.

"Right next to Joshua Bates," she said. The new boy walked quietly to his seat. He smiled at Joshua, but Joshua turned away before he had to smile back. Tommy Wilhelm made a fake kissing noise.

"Joshua," Mrs. Wooden announced, "seeing as Sean is new to Mirch Elementary, I think it would be nice if you showed him around."

Joshua groaned.

"What did you say, Joshua?"

"Yes, Mrs. Wooden."

"That's better."

The truth was, the very last thing in the world Joshua wanted was to be linked up with Sean O'Malley from New Jersey. Joshua had enough problems already. And now he had practically been forced to promise Mrs. Wooden he would be friends with the new boy, who was hardly more than three feet tall, as far as Joshua could tell, and, according to Tommy, who was an authority, a creep besides.

Soon after Mrs. Wooden began the lesson, Joshua was passed a note.

DEAR JOSHUA, it read, YOU HAVE THE CUTEST SMILE! It was signed, LOVE, SEAN. Across the bottom of the note someone had drawn a series of red hearts.

WHEN THE BELL RANG, Joshua waited impatiently while the red-haired midget slipped his Yankees jacket off the back of

his chair, took his empty book bag from under the desk, and picked up his Mickey Mouse lunchbox.

"I guess you just moved here," Joshua said. Sean O'Malley was so short that the top of his head came just to Joshua's shoulder.

"Yesterday," Sean said. "We used to live in Short Hills in a house with a swimming pool, but then my father got a new job."

Sean was bragging, Joshua thought, and he understood exactly how Sean felt. After all, Joshua had spent almost the whole of last year feeling just as small inside as Sean O'Malley in fact was.

"Not one of my old friends could possibly like me now that I've flunked," Joshua had told his mother.

"Pretend it doesn't matter, darling," his mother had said.

"But it does," Joshua complained. "It matters a lot."

He and Sean walked down the hall past the library, past the principal's office, past the other fifth graders on their way to math class. Joshua was certain the other children in the hall were laughing at the sight of him with this new boy and his Mickey Mouse lunchbox.

"My dad hasn't found a house with a swimming pool here," Sean said.

"We don't have a lot of swimming pools in D.C.," Joshua said. "Mostly in the summer we play baseball at the playground."

"I love baseball," Sean said. "I was a pitcher for my Little League team. I was actually the best pitcher in Short Hills. For my age, that is."

Tommy and Billy fell in step with Joshua and Sean.

"So you pitched for your Little League team?" Tommy asked.

Billy looked Sean up and down. "Are you sure it wasn't for the peewee league?"

"Leave him alone," Joshua warned, shouldering his way ahead, but Billy cut him off.

"What's your rush, Joshua?" Billy asked. His voice dropped to a whisper. "You and your girlfriend late for a date?" Joshua felt his face go very red and his fists tighten.

"Yeah, relax, Joshua," Tommy jumped in. "We just wanted to know if the new kid wanted to try out for our baseball team." Tommy turned to Sean. "How 'bout it, kid? You want to try out?"

"Sure," Sean said.

"Great," Tommy said. "We'll try you out at recess."

"Okay," Sean said.

Tommy and Billy walked off.

At that moment Joshua T. Bates knew in his heart the red-haired midget was finished as a fifth grader at Mirch Elementary.

MATH CLASS, as always, began right on time. But just as

Miss Lacey, pencil thin with a high fluty voice, clapped her hands to say that class would begin, Tommy Wilhelm called out, loud enough for the whole class to hear, "Awesome lunchbox, Sean. Where in the world did you get it?"

The class rumbled with laughter. Even Joshua laughed.

Miss Lacey clapped her hands again. "That's quite enough, class. Now let's begin."

Sean leaned over while Miss Lacey was writing fractions on the board for a math quiz.

"I hope we'll be good friends," he whispered to Joshua.

"Sure," Joshua said.

"My best friend in Short Hills was named Joshua, too," Sean said. "Maybe we'll get to be best friends."

Joshua felt doomed. He couldn't concentrate on the subtraction of fractions—or anything else for that matter. All he could think about were the plans the red-haired midget was making to be his best friend.

The fact was, Joshua already had a best friend. Andrew Porter. But that wasn't the real problem either. The real problem was Tommy Wilhelm. And the NOs. *Nerds Out*. It was a secret club Tommy had started after Joshua was promoted back into the fourth grade. "So we don't have to waste our time with nerds," Tommy had said.

Nerds like me, Joshua thought. And Joey Taggart, who had left Mirch Elementary, and Sammy Fox, who now went to a private school. Some nerds stayed, like Peter Sears, and simply made friends with other nerds or with kids in lower grades, which was practically the same thing. All because of Tommy Wilhelm and the NOs.

Joshua sighed. *It just isn't fair*.

Not surprisingly, when Miss Lacey handed back the quiz, Joshua had missed six out of ten problems and flunked.

"I don't believe you were thinking, Joshua Bates," Miss Lacey announced practically to the whole class.

Of course he wasn't thinking, Joshua thought miserably. His life was in peril, and this was only the beginning. Today he flunked a math quiz. Soon he would be flunking everything, even composition. Before he knew it, he'd be stuck in fifth grade. Probably forever. It was going to be just like last year. And all on account of the new kid.

THE BELL RANG for art before Miss Lacey could think of any more insults. Art was the one period of the day besides gym that made going to school tolerable. All the boys leaped out of their chairs and barreled out of math class down the back steps to art, except Joshua, who had to wait for Sean O'Malley. By the time he got to art class all the tables were taken, except, of course, the table in the back next to the window, where the nerds sat.

Joshua had to pass Tommy on the way to his seat.

"Hey, Bates," Tommy said, "I saved you a seat in the back with the nerds." A couple of the boys at Tommy's table laughed. "Or maybe you and your new girlfriend would rather sit with the other girls."

"Yeah, Sean," Billy Nickel said, "you and Joshua want to sit with your girlfriends?"

Before Joshua had a chance to do what he wanted to do, which was to knock Tommy Wilhelm on the head and Billy Nickel too while he was at it, Mr. Webb told him to quit talking and take his seat.

"But I didn't say anything," Joshua complained.

"Joshua," Mr. Webb said, "I don't want to have to tell you twice." He pointed his finger at the table in the back.

Tommy grinned. "Sucker."

Joshua, with Sean stuck to him like glue, walked to the table at the back of the room. On the way he passed Andrew Porter.

"I tried to save you a seat," Andrew whispered.

Joshua shrugged. He put his books down next to Brian Feller.

"Welcome to nerdville," Brian said, and quickly added, "that's a joke."

Joshua looked at him without smiling.

"TODAY," MR. WEBB SAID, "we will begin making bird feeders." Some children groaned. A few kids, girls probably, clapped. "And for this project," Mr. Webb went on, "we'll be using partners."

14

Joshua threw his hand into the air.

"Yes, Joshua," Mr. Webb said a little wearily. "What is it now?"

"I want Andrew Porter as a partner."

"Sorry, Joshua," Mr. Webb said. "Partners have already been assigned."

Darn, Joshua thought. Mr. Webb began to read off the partners from a list. With each name Joshua felt more and more sick. He knew his name would be called last.

Finally Mr. Webb put down the list and said, "Is there anyone whose name I haven't called?"

Reluctantly Joshua raised his hand.

"Joshua," Mr. Webb said. "Anyone else?"

The red-haired midget raised his hand. Mr. Webb looked out over the class, smiled, looked back down at his list, and looked up again.

"Sean O'Malley," Mr. Webb said. "The new boy."

"The new boy from New Girly," Tommy blurted.

"Joshua," Mr. Webb said, "I guess you and Sean are partners."

It was only the first Monday morning of the first week after vacation, and already the winter was looking long and dark for Joshua T. Bates.

chapter two

IT WAS WARM for January, damp but not raining, although the baseball field was wet and slippery. When the bell for recess rang, Joshua reluctantly followed Sean O'Malley to his locker, number 39—two down from Joshua's—and put on his own ski jacket and wool cap.

"I don't even have my baseball glove," Sean said to Joshua.

"Who does?" Joshua said. "It's a dumb idea to play baseball in the winter."

Andrew Porter walked up. "What's going on?" he asked Joshua.

"Tommy wants to see how Sean is as a pitcher," Joshua said.

"Sure," Andrew said. "I bet that's just what he has in mind." Andrew did not like Tommy Wilhelm either. He never had, but he steered clear of trouble. Because Andrew was so smart and got all A's, Tommy Wilhelm pretty much left him alone.

"You don't have to do everything Tommy says, you know," Andrew said.

"Of course I don't *have* to." Joshua boxed the locker door with his fist. "But we all do anyway."

He and Andrew had been friends nearly forever, ever since playgroup when they were two years old. And though Joshua had no memories of being two except one of eating marshmallows under the kitchen table, he felt as if he remembered Andrew always. They were not alike. Andrew studied all the time and played word games with his parents at dinner and read the newspaper every morning before he went to school, even the editorial page. Sometimes Joshua didn't know why they were still friends, since he and Andrew seemed so different. Some days Andrew even seemed grown up. But the fact was, they were best friends. When Joshua had flunked third grade, Andrew was the only person in the whole fourth grade who was willing to eat with him in the lunchroom. And that counted for everything.

"So you're not going to play?" Joshua asked Andrew.

"Nope," Andrew said. "I'm working in the library on a report on the Sioux so I can go to the movies tonight."

"Nerd," Joshua teased, and Andrew smiled.

"That was my best friend, Andrew Porter," Joshua said, leading Sean to the baseball field where Tommy Wilhelm and Billy Nickel were warming up. "He thinks it's a dumb idea to play baseball in the winter."

"So why are we doing it?" Sean asked, taking giant steps to keep up with Joshua as they walked across the field.

Because Andrew isn't captain of the world, Joshua thought. *Tommy Wilhelm is.* Joshua shrugged. He put his baseball cap on top of his wool cap, with the visor facing backward.

"I don't think Tommy Wilhelm likes me," Sean said, struggling to keep up.

"Tommy doesn't like a lot of guys," Joshua said.

"Does he like you?"

"We aren't best friends," Joshua said.

Tommy and Billy and a few other boys were standing at the equipment shed. Bats and baseball gloves were scattered on the ground.

"So you finally made it," Tommy said. "What were you doing? Putting on makeup or something?"

Billy laughed and blew a huge bubble with his gum. It exploded with a pop.

Joshua sighed and looked for a glove that might fit. He found one for Sean, too. "Here, Sean, try this."

"Teams are chosen except for you two guys," Tommy said. "And I choose the red-headed ace. What's your name again?"

"Sean." His voice was like a whisper.

"Yeah, right," Tommy said, sneering. "Shaaaawn." Tommy

tossed Sean a baseball. "Here you go, Ace. Let's see what you've got."

The glove Sean had on was about four sizes too big, and when he tried to catch the ball Tommy lobbed, the glove slid off his hand.

Tommy rolled his eyes and took his position as catcher behind home plate. Sean walked slowly to the pitcher's mound. He pounded his right hand into the glove several times.

Joshua sat down on the bench and immediately began to think of all the places he would rather be than on this bench watching the red-headed midget from New Jersey who as far as Joshua could tell was just about to have the most humiliating day of his life. Billy strolled over and plunked down on the bench next to Joshua.

"So your girlfriend is a pretty great pitcher," Billy said, and grinned. He blew a bubble the size of a soccer ball. Joshua poked it with his finger, and the bubble collapsed with a splat across Billy's face and hair.

"Hey!" Billy yelled. "What'd you do that for?"

"Gee," Joshua said innocently, "sorry. I guess I'm just clumsy."

"You will be sorry," Billy snarled, untangling strings of gum from his face and hair.

Tommy yelled for Billy to hurry up and start the game.

"Okay, okay," Billy said. "Jeez, what's the rush?" Billy went over to find a bat, found three, took several slow swings with each, selected one, slung it over his shoulder, and confidently strolled to home plate. He dug his toes into the dirt and took a few more swings. He smiled at Tommy.

"Ready," he said.

"Billy, what's all the pink crud in your hair?"

"Nothing," Billy said. "Let's play ball."

Tommy yelled out to Sean. "Okay, Ace!"

Tommy turned to Billy. "This is going to be a comedy show," he said, and they both laughed.

SEAN FINISHED his warmups. He waved to Tommy that he was ready. Turning to one side and bending slightly at the knees, just as a professional pitcher would do, he rolled into his windup. The ball sailed from his hand, hit the ground halfway to home plate, and rolled to a stop just in front of Billy's feet.

"Ball one," Tommy said.

Sean made a second pitch. This time the ball skipped behind Billy, out of the backstop, and down the grassy incline toward the basketball courts.

"Ball two!"

"Ball three!"

Billy yawned and pretended to fall asleep at the plate. He made exaggerated snoring sounds.

"Wake up, Billy!" Tommy yelled. "Here comes ball four!"

Sean coiled into his final windup. He threw the ball hard, but instead of crossing the plate the ball plopped harmlessly on Billy's shoulder.

Billy howled as if he had been hit by a Nolan Ryan fastball. He fell onto the ground, rolled back and forth, and grabbed his shoulder.

"Ball four! Take your base!"

Billy struggled to his feet, limped partway to first base, then broke into a skip.

"Hey, Ace," Billy yelled, "maybe you should try out for ballet instead of baseball. Maybe you're better with your feet than your hands!"

It was Joshua's turn to bat. Ordinarily Joshua loved to hit. He loved the feel of a bat in his hands and the hard crack of the ball as it made contact. But this time the bat felt awful. It was as heavy as lead.

Joshua stepped up to the plate. Sean curled into a windup and pitched.

"Ball one!"

"Ball two!" Billy Nickel stole second base. The left fielder sat down.

"Ball three!" The shortstop threw his glove in the air. Billy Nickel stole third base.

"Jeez!" Tommy yelled. "You must have the New Jersey record for balls!" Sean stared at the ground. He pounded his fist into his glove, adjusted his shoulders, and rubbed the ball on his pants.

"That's right, Ace," Billy called out, "you just need to settle down a bit."

Joshua cocked the bat on his shoulder. *Please*, he thought, *just one strike*.

The ball sailed toward the plate. For a split second it looked to Joshua as if it might be a strike. Joshua leaned into his swing. It was too late. The ball just seemed to die. It bounced about a foot in front of home plate and rolled lazily toward the backstop.

Tommy grinned meanly.

"Ball four!"

Right then Joshua would have liked to bop Tommy on the head with his bat so that Tommy would fall down unconscious for six weeks. But to the horror of Joshua T. Bates, the red-headed midget did the worst possible thing any humiliated boy could do. He burst into tears, threw down his glove, and walked off the field.

"You're not quitting, are you, Ace?" Tommy called out to him. "Just when you were getting warmed up?"

Everyone on the bench burst out laughing. Billy Nickel danced to home plate. Then he and Tommy and a few other boys jogged after Sean, who began walking faster and faster. Tommy grabbed Sean from behind.

Laughing and shouting, a circle of boys formed around

Sean, who was practically sobbing. Tommy pushed Sean, and he stumbled backward. Then another boy pushed Sean, who stumbled forward. Then he was pushed back again.

"Look at this!" Tommy shouted. "It's a human pinball machine!"

Joshua felt sick.

And then Sean ran. He broke free from the circle of boys and ran. Joshua watched and thought maybe he should run after Sean and explain that he understood about humiliation.

But he didn't.

ANDREW WAS in the library when Joshua went upstairs to put his coat away in his locker. Joshua went in, sat down, and put his head on the table next to his best friend.

"Guess what?" he said.

"What?" Andrew asked.

"The new boy can't pitch."

Andrew shrugged. "It's not the worst thing in the world."

"Nope," Joshua said. "I just feel sort of awful for him. Even though he is a nerd."

"I suppose any day now the NOs are going after him," Andrew said.

"They already have," Joshua said. "And I'm probably next."

"Tommy Wilhelm wouldn't go after you," Andrew said.

"And anyway, you already beat him up once. He wouldn't want to fight with you again."

"Maybe not," Joshua said, "but he didn't have so many friends last time." Joshua let out a deep sigh. "I can't explain it," he said. "It's just different now, not like it was in third grade."

Andrew nodded. "I know what you mean."

Joshua collected his books and went back to homeroom, where Sean O'Malley was sitting with his Yankees jacket on.

"Joshua," Mrs. Wooden said when he came into the classroom.

He walked over to her desk.

"I hope you are taking good care of Sean today."

"Yeah," he said. "I am. I will."

chapter three

AFTER LUNCH, Sean O'Malley asked Joshua if he could come over to Joshua's house after school.

"I guess," Joshua said, trying to think of an excuse, "although maybe I have a piano lesson. Meet me at the end of school and I'll tell you then."

"Great," Sean said. "I was afraid you might not like me after, you know, what happened."

"Oh, that was okay. Not everyone's a great pitcher."

"I don't mean about pitching. I mean the other."

"Yeah," Joshua began to say, but he didn't finish. The fact was, he felt sorry for Sean O'Malley, but he didn't approve of him crying at the baseball game.

"So see you later," Sean said. "We'll meet out front at three. Okay?"

"Okay," Joshua said.

The minute the bell rang for the end of school, and before Sean O'Malley probably had time to put on his Yankees jacket, Joshua bolted. He didn't even stop at his locker to get his books for math and language arts or even his coat. He flew down the front steps of Mirch, past a line of fifth-grade girls who screeched "Hunk!" when he raced by, down Thirty-fourth Street as fast as he could run to Lowell, and home. When he got there, Amanda was in the kitchen eating six chocolate chip cookies and a Kudos.

"Someone called," she said.

He took a cookie from her plate.

"Who?"

"Sean O'Malley. He said he'd call back. That he was supposed to come over to play today and you must have forgotten."

"You bet. That's just what I did. Forget." He opened the refrigerator door and took out a carton of milk. "So what'd you tell him?"

"To come on over. What else?"

"Creep." He took six, seven, eight cookies out of the jar.

The telephone rang, and Amanda went to answer it.

"If that's him," Joshua said, "tell him I'm not here."

Amanda had her hand on the receiver.

"But you *are* here, Josh," Amanda said slyly. "I see you standing right beside me eating a chocolate chip cookie, so you must be here."

Amanda picked up the receiver.

"Please, Amanda," Joshua begged. "This is not funny."

"Hello?"

Joshua froze. His mouth formed a silent "please."

"Joshua?" Amanda pretended to think. "Well, let me see." Amanda looked right at Joshua. "Joshua!" she called out sweetly. "Are you here?"

Joshua was frantically waving his hands no.

"Yes," Amanda said, "he's right here. Hold on a second."

Amanda was grinning like a witch. The receiver dangled from her right hand. "Surprise, Joshua. It's for you."

Joshua didn't remember what he said just then, but whatever it was, it wiped the smile right off Amanda's face.

"I'm telling!" Amanda screamed. "I'm telling Mom and Dad what you said, and probably you'll be grounded for life!"

Joshua ran down the hallway, barreled down the basement stairs, dove into the bathroom, and slammed the door. He heard footsteps and then Amanda's prissy voice outside the bathroom door.

"You're in big trouble now, Joshua T. Bates."

"Leave me alone, Amanda," Joshua moaned. "I'm sick. I'm throwing up." He growled deeply in his throat, coughed and spit a bit, then flushed the toilet.

"See. I told you I was sick."

"Are not."

"Am too!"

Amanda switched to her I'm-so-logical voice. "If you're so sick, why did you invite a friend over?"

"I didn't invite him over. And he's not my friend. He's a nerd and he's stuck to me."

"Well, here's a flash, Joshua. This *nerd* friend of yours is on his way over, and he should be here any minute."

Joshua sat down on the edge of the tub and waited until he thought Amanda had finally lost interest in bothering him, which knowing Amanda might take all night and most of the next day. He thought he finally heard her footsteps down the hall, listened at the door, opened it, and quietly sneaked up the stairs and into his bedroom.

He closed the door behind him, climbed up into his bunk bed, and slipped the covers over his head.

And that is exactly where he was, lying nose to nose with Egypt, his stuffed crocodile, burning with shame at his terrible behavior, when he heard the soft voice of his mother talking to Georgianna on her way upstairs.

"Amanda tells me you're ill," his mother said. "Actually she tells me you are pretending to be ill." His mother was standing at the door to his room, but he didn't look down from his bunk.

"I am ill," Joshua said. "Very."

She walked across his room, climbed the ladder of his bunk bed, and sat down at the foot of the bed so he could just see her over the head of his crocodile.

He didn't want any more trouble than he'd already had, and he knew that if Sean O'Malley appeared at their front door he was doomed. His mother would ask Sean in, take him to the kitchen for chocolate chip cookies and hot cocoa, set him up in the television room in front of the TV or take him to the old playroom in the basement, where there was a Ping-Pong table, or invite him to come to the study to read some books and stay for dinner, spend the night, move in. That's the kind of mother she was, which was swell most of the time. But not today.

"What's really the matter?" she asked, rubbing his arm.

"I am not physically sick, if that's what you mean."

"Then what?"

"I'm sick with worry," he admitted.

"That's what I thought. Are you having trouble with math?"

"I got a D on a quiz today." His mother frowned. Joshua added quickly, "But that's not the real trouble. The real trouble is a new boy came to Mirch today from New Jersey, and he's stuck to me."

"But that's very nice. It means he likes you, darling."

"Believe me, it's not very nice at all. It's a disaster. It could mean the end of my life in fifth grade."

"No, Joshua. You are stronger than that. You proved that when you flunked third grade."

"You don't understand, Mom," Joshua said.

Joshua would have liked to have told his mother about

Tommy Wilhelm and the NOs and about what it meant to be a nerd or even a friend of a nerd. But she wouldn't understand that because she was a mother, and besides, if she heard about the NOs she'd call Mrs. Wooden and Andrew Porter's mother and probably Tommy Wilhelm's mother and certainly the principal. Then there'd be real trouble.

He was just about to tell her why the new boy was ridiculed when the doorbell rang.

"Joshy," Amanda called up in her singsong voice, "someone's here to see you."

"Brother," Joshua said, and covered his face with Egypt. "Please tell him I'm sick."

His mother climbed down the ladder.

"And please drown Amanda in the sink."

IN LESS THAN a minute, in less time than it would have taken Joshua to fly under his covers, there was the red-haired midget standing in the doorway to his room, still clutching the Mickey Mouse lunchbox.

"Hi," he said in a very small voice. "I guess you forgot me."

"I'm sort of sick," Joshua said.

"I know. Your sister told me. So I thought we could just play quietly on your bed." He started up the ladder. "When I was little, that's what my mother told me to do if I was sick. Just play quietly on my bed."

31

Sean sat down at the end of Joshua's bed, took off his Yankees jacket, opened his book bag, and took out a small box.

"Do you like cards or games?" he asked. "I've got both."

Joshua felt defeated. "Games, I guess."

AT FIVE Mrs. Bates came in with Georgianna. "What time does your family expect you home?" she asked Sean.

"They don't," Sean said. "It's only my father anyway, and he works all the time. My mother lives in California now. She says she likes the climate better." He scrambled down the ladder. "I could have dinner with you, if that's what you're wondering."

Mrs. Bates laughed.

"Actually I wasn't wondering," she said. "But you're welcome to have dinner just tonight. Generally on school nights no one comes to dinner, but since you're new in Washington, we'll make an exception."

"I'm a little sick, remember?" Joshua said, but he knew he had lost.

"I can help," Sean said. "I'll set the table if you want. Or help stir something." And he was off down the stairs to the kitchen.

"Thanks a lot, Mom," Joshua said crossly.

"I couldn't help it, darling. He breaks my heart."

"Well, he doesn't break my heart," Joshua said.

"Besides, it's only for tonight," she said.

"Just wait and see," Joshua predicted. "He's never going to leave now." He crawled under the covers and put Egypt over his face to shut out the world.

chapter four

THE RED-HAIRED MIDGET left not long after dinner. His father, a small red-haired man, excessively shy and polite, rolled up in a shiny blue sports car. He thanked Mr. and Mrs. Bates, thanked Joshua, and said how very happy he was that Sean had found a friend—a "best" friend, Sean corrected—so quickly. He also said he hoped the two would spend a lot of time together because of course Sean missed his mother and his old friends in Short Hills, New Jersey. To Joshua, Sean seemed very happy. He seemed not to have noticed for a second that Joshua would have gladly sent him express delivery back to Short Hills.

"Next time I'll do the dishes," Sean said.

Next time? Joshua instantly felt his stomach go weak.

Joshua's father laughed when Sean mentioned the dishes and said, "That won't be necessary," and even told Sean he was welcome "anytime."

35

"Except school nights," Joshua added hastily. "And certain weekends, maybe."

The red-haired midget's father first shook hands with Mr. Bates and then with Mrs. Bates. Then Sean shook hands with Mr. Bates and Mrs. Bates, who seemed surprised at his formality.

Finally the front door closed and the nightmare named Sean O'Malley was gone. At least, Joshua thought, for now.

"He seems like a fine boy," his father said on the way to the kitchen. "Very polite."

Joshua collapsed with relief onto the living room sofa. Amanda was helping Georgianna balance her ice cream cone.

"I don't think Sean is such a nerd," Amanda said. "In fact, I think he may even be kind of cute."

Joshua scowled.

"He seems halfway intelligent, at least."

"Big deal," Joshua snapped. "Being smart doesn't automatically make you popular. Look at you, for example."

"Very funny, Mr. Maturity. I guess not everyone proves how popular he is by flunking third grade."

Joshua felt his cheeks burn. "I was promoted, in case you forgot," Joshua said.

Georgianna began to whimper. A ball of chocolate ice cream lay at her feet.

"Oh, brother," Joshua said. He jumped up and stormed into the kitchen.

"He's a total nerd," he said crossly to no one in particular.

"Who's a nerd?" Mr. Bates asked. He and Mrs. Bates were at the sink doing the dinner dishes.

"Can I have a soda?" Joshua asked.

"No," Mr. Bates said. "And who's a nerd?"

Joshua was too depressed to lie. "Sean O'Malley."

"What do you mean by a nerd?"

Joshua sat down sulkily at the kitchen table. "Someone who doesn't fit in. Who's not exactly regular."

"No one is regular, Josh," Mrs. Bates said. "Everybody has trouble fitting in at some time. You of all people should know that."

"You know what I mean," Joshua said. "I'm sure there were nerds when you were my age."

"I suppose I was one," Mr. Bates said. "Most of the good students were thought to be nerds when I was your age."

"Well, I don't want to be a nerd, which is lucky, because I'm a terrible student," Joshua said. "And Sean O'Malley is a nerd."

"That doesn't give you the okay to be rude to him, Joshua," Mrs. Bates said.

"You were unkind to him, Josh," Mr. Bates said. "I was very surprised."

"He didn't notice."

"He noticed." Mr. Bates had a certain fierceness about him that made his children wary. "He was simply too polite to say so."

"I think," his mother said, "you might even owe Sean an apology."

"For what?"

"For being rude and inconsiderate," his father said.

"I didn't even want him over," Joshua complained. His voice was tense with anger and frustration. "I said I was sick, and anyway it was Amanda who answered the phone and asked him over. Why not make her apologize?"

"Because he's *your* friend, Joshua."

Sometimes it felt to Joshua as if his father never heard anything he said.

"He's not my friend! He's trying to take over my life!"

Mrs. Bates sat down at the table next to Joshua.

"Listen, darling. We're not saying you have to be friends with everyone," she said to him.

"Well, then I don't want to be friends with Sean O'Malley." Joshua folded his arms across his chest.

"But," his mother said, "he deserves to be treated with respect. Even if you do think he's a nerd."

Joshua was too exhausted to argue. The fact was, his mother was wrong. It did matter if you were a nerd or not. Tommy Wilhelm and the NOs were proof of that.

"It's just not fair," Joshua said.

"Maybe not," Mr. Bates said, "but that's the way it is."

IT WAS ONLY seven o'clock, but Joshua decided to put on his pajamas, brush his teeth, and climb into bed instead of watching TV. He lay on the top bunk in the dark, staring at the ceiling, thinking about nothing except how unfair it all was. Maybe his father was right, Joshua thought. Maybe *that's just the way it is*. Maybe there would always be guys like Tommy Wilhelm and Billy Nickel and the NOs in life, and Joshua would just have to get used to it. He'd be a forty-year-old man walking down the street minding his own business when a forty-year-old Tommy Wilhelm would step in front of him. Joshua rolled onto his side and wondered what else could possibly go wrong. And then he remembered. He was failing math.

After a while his mother came in and said Andrew Porter was on the phone. Andrew and Joshua talked on the phone almost every night, and had for as long as Joshua could remember. But tonight Joshua didn't feel like talking to Andrew.

"Tell him I'm sick."

"Okay, Joshua, if that's what you want."

"That's what I want."

His mother left, and Joshua lay for a long time thinking. It felt as if the whole world were pressing in on him.

There was a light knock on his door. His mother came in and said if he was willing, she would like to talk to him.

"Nope," he said. "I'm not."

"I wonder if you'd explain to me why you are so worried about nerds, Joshua," his mother said. "You never worried about things like this when you were little."

"Of course I didn't," Joshua said. "I was too young to know the difference. But now I know the difference, and so does everyone else in the fifth grade."

"You're young and healthy and smart and a good athlete. You should be having a wonderful time in fifth grade, darling."

"Well, I'm not having a wonderful time, and you're the only one who thinks I'm smart."

Amanda came into Joshua's room and flicked on the light. Her hair was frizzed, and she wore her cheerleading uniform.

"Amanda!" Joshua said. He pulled Egypt over his eyes.

"Sorrrrry," she said. "Anyway, you have a phone call from Tommy Wilhelm."

Joshua sat up. Tommy Wilhelm had never called before. In spite of himself, Joshua felt flattered. But he was also suspicious.

"He says," Amanda repeated in her best imitation Tommy Wilhelm voice, "that it's *very* important."

Joshua hesitated. What if Tommy had somehow found out that Sean had come to dinner at the Bateses' house? But

40

how would he have found out? Then why would he be calling?

Joshua felt dizzy.

"Well?" Amanda said.

"Tell him I'm sick."

"How original." Amanda smirked. "Tell him yourself. I'm not your secretary."

"Amanda," Mrs. Bates said.

"Oh, all right," Amanda said, and left.

"I didn't know you and Tommy Wilhelm were friends," his mother said.

"We're not."

"Then why is he calling, Joshua?" she asked.

Joshua shrugged.

"Is he still as unpleasant as he used to be?" Mrs. Bates asked.

"Worse," Joshua admitted. "He gets more awful every day."

Amanda came back into the room.

"He says the important thing is about a club. A *secret* club," she said dramatically. "He's sure you'll be able to get up out of your sickbed to hear about a *secret* club."

Mrs. Bates frowned.

"What's this about a secret club?" she asked Joshua.

Joshua felt defensive.

"Who knows?" he said. "Everything Tommy does is secret. He's practically a professional criminal."

Mrs. Bates told Amanda to tell Tommy Wilhelm that Joshua

was doing homework and could not come to the phone.

"I don't like secret clubs," Mrs. Bates told Joshua. "And I certainly hope you would never join one."

"Never," Joshua promised.

"I've never liked Tommy Wilhelm." Mrs. Bates seemed relieved.

She kissed Joshua on the forehead.

"Sleep well, darling," she said. "Maybe by tomorrow morning things will seem much better. You'll walk to school with Andrew and you probably won't even remember why you were so upset tonight."

On her way out she flicked off the bedroom light and started to shut the door.

"Don't," Joshua said.

"I thought the hall light kept you awake."

"I don't plan to go to sleep," Joshua said. He turned over on his side. "I wish I didn't care whether or not I was popular. Like Andrew. He doesn't care."

"Andrew is a different person," his mother said. "Books matter more to him than people."

"I matter to him."

"Of course you do. I mean people in general don't matter as much to Andrew as they do to you. You need to feel as if you have a lot of friends. Andrew is perfectly happy just to have you."

"He's even kind of a nerd," Joshua said. "Not as bad as

Sean and some of the real nerds who wear their pants up to their chests and their hair slicked down. But since it doesn't matter to Andrew whether or not he's popular, no one notices that he's a nerd."

"Maybe you could try and be a bit more like Andrew," she suggested.

"Maybe," Joshua said sadly. The fact was, to Joshua T. Bates fitting in mattered a great deal.

Joshua had trouble falling asleep. Even after Amanda finished trying on every single outfit in her closet and turned off the hall light so she could talk in the dark and in secret to her eighth-grade boyfriend, Joshua tossed and turned. All he could think about was Tommy Wilhelm's telephone call.

Tommy had either called to ask him to join the NOs, which was very unlikely, or else he, Joshua T. Bates, was about to be the new victim of Nerds Out. Either way, his life at Mirch Elementary was going to change.

Joshua woke up early, even before the sun had lightened the morning to day. He was full of trepidation, an unfamiliar sense of doom, not the sad humiliation he had felt in the third grade but a feeling altogether different and disturbing. He wanted to call Andrew, but it was only six o'clock. He got up, made his bed, which he simply never did unless he was asked, took a shower, which he also never did unless he was asked, went downstairs, walked his dog, Plutarch, around the block, fed him and Marmalade the cat, poured a bowl of Special K and a glass of orange juice, and by the time his father's alarm clock rang was ready to go to school.

"Joshua," his mother said groggily when she came downstairs in her blue robe, "what are you doing up so early?"

"I don't know," Joshua said. "Nothing, I guess."

His mother got apple juice from the refrigerator and made coffee.

"I fed Marmalade and Plutarch and walked him."

"And you've eaten?"

"Yup."

"You've had orange juice?"

"Yup."

Mrs. Bates sat down beside Joshua and took his wrist in her hand. "I'm sorry about last night, Joshua."

Joshua shrugged. "No problem."

"Are you feeling better?"

"Yeah, sure. I guess."

"That's good. And Joshua?" She folded her other hand over his and patted it. "Try to be nice to Sean O'Malley today. Okay?"

"Sure, Mom." Joshua forced himself to sound convincing, but even to him his words sounded lopsided.

Mrs. Bates got up to pour some coffee.

Since he'd left his new jacket at school, Joshua put on his old ski jacket with sleeves that came halfway down his arms, slipped his arms through the straps of his book bag, and put three Kudos in his pocket for a snack.

"I've been thinking that maybe I could change schools," he said matter-of-factly. "Joey Taggart did. He changed to Horace Mann because the art is better."

Mrs. Bates sipped her coffee.

"Horace Mann isn't in our district, darling."

"Joey didn't move. He still lives on Woodley Road. His parents just decided to send him to Mann because of the art."

"And you want to go because of the art?"

"Right."

"I didn't know you had such an interest in art, Joshua, but we'll look into it. Maybe you could take art lessons at the community center."

"Maybe," he said, and started out the door. "Also, I hate Miss Lacey."

"I know you do, darling, but there will always be teachers you don't like, no matter what."

Not if I never go back to school, Joshua thought. Not if I moved to Africa.

"I just feel pressure," Joshua said. "I can't explain it." He kissed his mother good-bye.

It was beginning to snow, a light thin snow, almost invisible, damp on his cheeks as Joshua walked quickly down Lowell to Thirty-fourth and turned left at Veazy Street.

chapter five

ANDREW LIVED a very quiet and orderly life with his father, who was a doctor, and his mother, who was also a doctor, no other children, no dogs, no cats, no birds, and one fish called Fish, which was the only pet Andrew's mother permitted in the house because she disliked confusion. Which is why Andrew loved the friendly disorder of the Bateses' lively house.

Joshua Bates turned the corner of Thirty-fourth Street to Veazy. Joshua sat down on the curb and waited for Andrew. After a while, Andrew strolled up as usual, wearing his snow jacket and wool cap and mittens, which he never misplaced, his waterproof book bag full of completed homework neatly done and on time, his Wellington boots, and his flute case. Andrew Porter was practically the only boy in fifth grade who could get away with taking flute lessons without being ridiculed. Once Billy Nickel tried to tease Andrew by asking, "Wouldn't you rather take ballet than flute?"

"I like the flute," Andrew had said coolly. "I've never tried ballet." And Billy never brought up the subject again.

Even so, Andrew wasn't perfect. Even he worried about Tommy Wilhelm and Billy Nickel because, as he had said to Joshua many times, they were mean and would do anything to anyone. But Andrew didn't let them know it.

"You'll never guess who called me last night," Joshua said, falling into step with Andrew.

"Madonna," Andrew said.

"I wish. Guess again."

"Wilhelm."

Joshua stopped dead in his tracks. "Right. Absolutely right. How did you guess?"

"He's going to do something to the new boy," Andrew said. "It's too much of an opportunity."

"Or to me."

"Why you?"

"He's wanted to do something to me for a long time and now I'm the new baby-sitter for Sean O'Malley. He's up for trouble."

"Maybe he wants to ask you to join the NOs."

"You bet."

Tommy Wilhelm was already at Mirch, calmly sitting on the roof of the equipment shed with Billy Nickel and W.V. Wood, when Joshua and Andrew arrived.

"So look who's here," Joshua whispered to Andrew as they passed by at a distance.

"With W.V.," Andrew said. "Do you think W.V.'s a member of the NOs?"

"Well, he's a total jerk. So probably."

W.V. was a small, skinny spider monkey of a boy who wore his brother's too-large hand-me-down clothes. He fought with just about everybody except Tommy, and in spite of his size nobody picked on him, even the older boys. In first grade he had picked a fight on the playground with Andrew—had thrown him down on his back behind the shed and spit in his face.

"You should tell," Joshua had said that afternoon as they walked home together.

"No way," Andrew said. "And don't you ever tell either."

Since that time Andrew did not speak to W.V., and if they happened to be at the same lunch table or in the same homeroom or science class, Andrew moved to a chair as far away as possible.

"Josh," W.V. shouted from the top of the shed. "Come on over."

"Later," Joshua said.

"I've got something to tell you," Tommy Wilhelm said.

"Tell me in class," Joshua said. He turned to Andrew. "Let's beat it."

"Fine with me," Andrew said.

They walked up the back steps into Mirch Elementary, past the principal's office, the nurse's office, and the teachers' lounge to their lockers, side by side, and near Johnny Hayes, called Jell-O because he was big and fleshy with a belly that hung over his belt. Jell-O was famous at Mirch for his obnoxious behavior and his loud voice, but he was a very good student, so the teachers liked him even if the students didn't. Or at least most of the students didn't like him, but it was well known that he was a friend of Tommy Wilhelm's.

When Andrew and Joshua walked down the corridor, Jell-O Hayes was on his knees, his head in his locker and his very large rear end in the corridor.

Joshua opened his locker, stuffed his jacket and snow hat into the bottom, got his language arts book from the shelf, took the cookies out of his lunch, and put the lunchbox on top of his clothes.

"So what's up?" Jell-O Hayes asked, slamming the door of his locker.

"Not much," Joshua said.

"Did you finish your science report?" Jell-O asked.

Joshua shrugged.

"I heard Mr. Kirby say it was late."

50

"Well, I didn't hear him," Joshua said. He put his book bag over his shoulder.

"Did Tommy get in touch with you?"

"Nope," Joshua said.

"I thought he called you," Jell-O said. "He told me he was going to call you last night."

"Maybe he did," Joshua said. "I was sick."

"Yeah? What with?" Jell-O asked.

"Scurvy," Joshua said.

"No kidding? Where did you get it?" Jell-O said.

"India. I went to India for Christmas vacation to see friends."

"That's funny. I didn't think you had friends." Jell-O began to laugh so hard his belly rumbled.

Joshua rolled his eyes and followed Andrew down the corridor to their classroom.

"I can't stand him," Joshua said.

"But I wouldn't want to cross him," Andrew said.

"Or have him sit on me." Joshua and Andrew laughed.

"Do you think he's a member of the NOs too?" Joshua asked.

"Maybe," Andrew said. "Probably."

THE FIRST BELL rang just as Andrew and Joshua walked into the classroom. Joshua slipped into his seat. He hadn't seen the red-haired midget before class and hadn't noticed him when he and Andrew walked in.

51

Maybe he'd moved again, Joshua thought happily. Maybe moving vans arrived at the O'Malley house in the middle of the night. Maybe Sean had moved to California to be with his mother in a house filled with red-haired nerds.

Maybe it wouldn't be such a bad day after all, Joshua thought. He was still flunking math. Tommy Wilhelm hated him, or maybe he didn't. Joshua wasn't sure. But at least he seemed to be free of the red-haired midget.

Then he felt a few tugs on the back of his shirt and a tiny whisper of a voice.

"Hi, Sean," Joshua said wearily. "What's up?" The light sensation Joshua had begun to feel turned heavy as lead.

"Someone stole my lunchbox," Sean said.

For a terrible moment Joshua thought the red-haired midget was going to start crying again.

"I was standing at my locker just a minute ago and it was on the floor, and I was putting my things away and when I looked down it was gone," he said. But Sean didn't cry. He just looked small. Even smaller than normal.

"What's the big deal, Sean? You can have some of my lunch." Joshua was practically whispering so as not to be overheard talking with the red-haired midget. "I have tunafish. You like tunafish?"

"Yeah," Sean said, and shrugged. "It's okay."

"Great," Joshua said. "We'll split my sandwich."

"It's not just the lunchbox," Sean said. "My dad gave me

a bunch of money to buy school supplies and stuff, and now—" Sean's voice seemed to flutter and tears welled up in his eyes.

"Class is about to start," Joshua said. "We'll talk later. Okay?"

AFTER CLASS, Joshua left with Andrew.

"You know about Sean's lunchbox?"

"I heard about it," Andrew said.

"The NOs?"

"Who else?"

Joshua sighed. He could see it as plain as day. This was going to be a very long week. A very, very long week.

chapter six

IN THE CORRIDOR on the way to math, Tommy Wilhelm pulled Joshua aside. "I've got to talk to you at recess."

"Maybe," Joshua said. "I may be on the playground."

"Just be at the equipment shed at recess, Bates. I mean it."

"I'll try," Joshua said.

But the wet snow had turned to a steady rain, so recess was indoors—in the library or the lunchroom or the gym. Joshua decided to do his math homework in the library during recess, so he had an excuse to avoid the red-haired midget and he didn't have to have a conversation with Tommy Wilhelm, who, after all, wouldn't be caught dead in the library. Joshua either, for that matter.

During art W.V. had gotten up to sharpen his pencil. The

sharpener was in the back of the room, behind the table where the nerds sat. On his way back, W.V. locked his foot around a leg of Sean's stool and pulled, and Sean crashed to the floor.

The whole class burst into laughter. W.V. even made a big show of pretending to apologize.

"Here," W.V. said, holding out his hand, "let me help you up." Sean reached for his hand, but W.V. pushed Sean down again.

"Oops," W.V. said.

By this time Mr. Webb was standing over Sean. He helped Sean up and ordered W.V. back to his seat.

"And be more careful next time," he told W.V.

"Gee, Mr. Webb," W.V. pleaded innocently, "he was so small I didn't even see him sitting there." W.V. winked at Tommy as he went by, and they exchanged low-fives. "Good job, W.V.," Tommy said.

Sean was silent all through art, even when the class broke up into partners and he and Joshua were standing side by side nailing together the sides of their bird feeder.

Joshua kept his eye on the clock. He didn't want the bell for recess to ring while he was with Sean. Then he would probably get stuck with him on the way out. As soon as the bell rang, Joshua gathered together his books and things and rushed away. As he left, however, he noticed Tommy and a few other boys hanging around just outside the classroom door. Sean walked out, his head down. Tommy stuck out his leg while another boy pushed Sean from behind. Sean stumbled and fell. His books went flying across the hallway. One of the boys walked over to Sean, who was sprawled on his stomach, and pushed his foot into Sean's back, pinning him.

"He's as tiny as a bug."

The boys laughed hysterically.

"A jerk bug," another boy said.

Tommy noticed Joshua standing off to the side. Sean was struggling to get up, but the more he wiggled, the harder the boy pushed his foot down. Tommy jerked his chin toward Joshua.

"You got a problem with this, Bates?"

"Maybe he wants to come to his girlfriend's rescue," W.V. said.

"No way," Tommy kidded W.V. "Even Bates isn't that stupid." Tommy turned to Joshua. "Are you, Bates?"

Joshua was already gone.

AT LUNCH Sean was sitting alone at a table when Joshua and Andrew came into the lunchroom.

"I guess we should sit with him," Andrew said.

"We have to," Joshua said. "I told him I'd share my tuna-fish sandwich."

"Okay," Andrew said.

"But we won't make a habit of it or anything," Joshua said. Andrew agreed.

They sat down next to Sean and Joshua opened his lunchbox, unwrapped his sandwich, and gave Sean half, plus some carrots and a pear.

"Thanks," Sean said.

" 'S okay," Joshua said. The lunchroom was getting crowded. Joshua couldn't be sure, but it seemed as if everyone was staring at him. Even the little kids Joshua remembered from when he flunked and who looked up to him for the most part were staring. And probably thinking, "Joshua T. Bates . . . the nerd."

Joshua slid down in his chair. Andrew and Sean were talking about museums.

"There aren't many museums in New Jersey," Sean said.

Andrew was munching on his sandwich.

"Washington has tons of museums," Andrew said. "But I think the National Air and Space Museum is my favorite. It's really neat. You should go."

There was a commotion at a table at the back of the room. It was Tommy and Billy and some other boys. Oh, no, Joshua thought. W.V. was headed right toward them. He was carrying his tray, and a couple of times he looked back at Tommy, grinning.

Joshua tried to slide even farther down in his chair. He would have liked to slide right through the floor, through the center of the earth, and on to China.

Andrew was just telling Sean about his plans to visit Mount Vernon when the tray that W.V. was carrying tipped and spilled on Sean O'Malley's head. Two orange juices and a glass of chocolate milk dripped down his shoulders. Tomato sauce and lasagna plastered his red hair. Corn drizzled down the back of his neck.

"I'm sorry," W.V. said. "Jeez. I thought I had it balanced. I'm *reaaally* sorry, Sean. I'm just *sooo* clumsy."

Andrew and Joshua looked over and exchanged embarrassed glances.

Sean reached up to his head and ran his hand through the lasagna. " 'S okay," Sean whispered.

"Here," W.V. offered, "I'll get you a napkin."

W.V. picked up a paper napkin from Andrew's tray and roughly rubbed the lasagna and tomato sauce all over Sean's head and down the back of his neck.

Joshua could hear Tommy and Billy Nickel laughing. He shot up from his seat.

"See you in a minute," he called to Andrew, and ran out the back door of the lunchroom, up the stairs, and down the corridor, and burst into the boys' bathroom next to the principal's office. He was either laughing or crying, he couldn't tell which.

Andrew had followed. Joshua heard the door open, and there was Andrew in the mirror over the sinks where Joshua was rinsing his face.

"Poor Sean," Andrew said. "I wish I had the guts to tell."

"You saw W.V. tip his tray?"

"Sure," Andrew said. "Didn't you?"

"I didn't need to see it happen," Joshua said.

Just then Sean O'Malley flew into the boys' room, covered with juice and chocolate milk and lasagna.

"I guess you saw what happened," he said, his voice shaky.

"Yeah," Joshua said. "Maybe you could wash most of that gunk out."

"And I have some extra clothes in my locker. You know, if you'd like to borrow them," Andrew said.

"Maybe." Sean took off his shirt and put it under the faucet.

Andrew left and came back with a flannel shirt and sweater. "I don't know what you can do about the stuff in your hair," he said.

"It's probably going to stick and be there all day," Sean said, putting his head under the faucet. Then he put on Andrew's shirt, which was huge on him.

The boys' room filled up quickly then—Tommy Wilhelm and W.V. and Billy Nickel and Jell-O Hayes came in from the lunchroom and stood around trading baseball cards, talking about their plans after school, pretending that nothing out of the ordinary had happened. Sean started toward the door.

"See you later, Sean," Tommy said ominously.

Then Tommy said, "Listen, Josh, why don't you come over after school today?"

"Can't," Joshua said, thinking quickly. "I've got a dentist's appointment."

"After the dentist's appointment," Tommy said. "Do you know where I live?"

"Nope," Joshua lied. He knew exactly where Tommy Wilhelm lived, but he had never been invited to Tommy's and he certainly didn't want Tommy Wilhelm to think he had any interest in where he lived.

"My address is 4256 Chesapeake," Tommy said. "Some of the guys are coming over to play Nintendo."

"Maybe," Joshua said, and he left the boys' bathroom as the bell for fifth period was ringing.

Sean was sitting on the floor in front of his locker.

"Hi," Joshua said, pretending it was a perfectly ordinary day.

Sean had a piece of paper in his lap. "Look what I got," he said, and handed the paper to Joshua. On the paper was a crude drawing of a ballet dancer and a note: DEAR SEANY, I JUST LOVE TO WATCH YOU DO BALLET. LOVE FOREVER, MILDRED SHOETREE.

"They hate me," Sean said.

Joshua had a sinking feeling in his stomach. "You've been kind of unlucky, that's all," he said.

"It's more than bad luck," Sean said. He stood up, opened his locker, and began pulling books out. Just then the door to the boys' room opened and Tommy Wilhelm walked out with Jell-O Hayes and Billy Nickel and W. V. Wood.

"Yeah. Well, see you," Joshua said, heading down the corridor in a hurry. And when Sean called "Wait for me," he pretended not to hear.

chapter seven

Mirch Elementary School was a rectangular brick building with green doors and a chain-link fence around the playground, similar in look to most public grammar schools everywhere. Except on the roof of Mirch, just above the center doors and reachable by the window in the main hall, was a modern sculpture in bright yellows and blues and reds done by one of the parents. At three o'clock on Tuesday afternoon, even though the rain was falling in a steady sheet and the sky was gray, the children just dismissed for the day could easily see that in the long red arm of the sculpture on the roof was a Mickey Mouse lunchbox.

Tommy Wilhelm was sitting on the top cement step with Billy Nickel and Jell-O Hayes in their yellow slickers when Joshua ran out the front door of the school in a particular hurry.

"Did you see the new decoration?" Tommy asked as Joshua passed by. He pointed to the sculpture on the roof.

"You know whose that is?"

"Sure," Joshua said, trying to be very casual about it. "Sean's."

"Maybe he had plans to eat lunch on the roof," Jell-O said.

"You bet," Joshua said.

"Did you see Sean?" Tommy asked Joshua. "He'll be very glad to know we've located his lunchbox."

"Yeah. I imagine he will," Joshua said, ignoring Tommy's question. "That was swell of you, Tommy," he added sarcastically.

He left quickly and walked over to the flagpole, where he met Andrew Porter every afternoon after school, which is where the principal found him.

Mr. Barnes was young for a principal and good-humored. He played soccer with the fifth and sixth graders in the fall and baseball in the spring. He had a picnic at his house every June for the whole sixth grade, and once during the winter he rented a movie theater and asked all of Mirch Elementary to come to the movies. He had a reputation for being fair, and ever since Joshua's troubles in third grade Mr. Barnes had shown a particular interest in him. This afternoon, however, Mr. Barnes was not in a good humor.

"Joshua Bates!" he called.

Joshua walked over, his heart in his feet.

64

"I need to speak to you right away in my office."

"I have a dentist's appointment," Joshua said.

"Your dentist's appointment will have to wait," Mr. Barnes said, going back inside.

Billy Nickel whistled.

"This sounds like a big deal," Tommy Wilhelm said.

"If you need any help, let us know," Jell-O said.

"I'll punch him out if he gives you any trouble," W.V. said.

On his way to Mr. Barnes's office Joshua passed Andrew.

"I'm in big trouble," Joshua said.

"What's up?"

"Mr. Barnes wants to see me in his office pronto."

"You think it's about Sean?" Andrew asked.

"Of course it's about Sean," Joshua said. "Unless it's about math, which I'm flunking."

"Well, someone stole his Yankees jacket."

"Great," Joshua said. "And his Mickey Mouse lunchbox is on the roof of the building. Wait for me at the flagpole," he added. "I've got to get over to the principal's office before I'm in worse trouble."

MR. BARNES was waiting for Joshua in his office. He shut the door and told Joshua to take a seat in the chair across from his desk.

"You know why you're here?"

"I'm flunking math."

"Maybe you are," Mr. Barnes said. "But that's not why you're here."

Joshua knew without having to guess.

"Sean O'Malley."

"Exactly."

Mr. Barnes had a large desk with stacks of paper in rows, gold-framed color photographs of his children, a picture of himself standing on the bow of a sailboat, a statue of a dog done by a student in art class, and papers in a box that said IMPORTANT. From the top of that box he took a large folded note and gave it to Joshua.

"As you may have noticed, a lunchbox is hanging on the sculpture on the roof of the building."

"I saw."

"Presumably it belongs to Sean O'Malley."

"Yes, it does."

"I received this letter shortly after lunch," Mr. Barnes said. "Why don't you read it."

The note, which was printed in block letters, said: DEAR MR. BARNES, SEAN O'MALLEY, THE NEW BOY IN FIFTH GRADE, IS BEING PERSECUTED BY JOSHUA BATES. WE HAPPENED TO SEE JOSHUA STEAL SEAN'S LUNCHBOX AND HANG IT ON THE SCULPTURE ON THE ROOF. It was signed, FRIENDS OF SEAN O'MALLEY.

"That's a lie," Joshua said. His heart was beating so hard it felt as if it had jumped into his mouth.

"I understand Mrs. Wooden asked you to keep an eye out for Sean," Mr. Barnes said.

"She asked me to show him around, if that's what you mean."

Mr. Barnes laced his fingers together and leaned across his desk.

"Joshua, I want you to tell me what has been going on with Sean O'Malley."

"A lot has happened," Joshua said. "He was tripped in the hall. Someone pulled his stool out from under him in art class." Joshua was uncomfortable. He itched all over and tiny beads of sweat were rolling down his back.

"And?" Mr. Barnes prompted.

"I guess someone spilled a tray on him at lunch. And someone stole his jacket."

Mr. Barnes was not smiling.

"But it wasn't me," Joshua said. "I promise it wasn't me."

"Is that what you think I think?" Mr. Barnes asked.

Joshua wasn't exactly sure.

"I guess not," he said.

Mr. Barnes sighed.

"Joshua, you're the only student who has been with Sean on a regular basis. If anybody might know what is going on, you would. Now I want you to tell me who you think is responsible for all this."

Joshua didn't enjoy the idea of lying to Mr. Barnes. But confessing about the NOs would be worse.

"Who, Joshua?" Mr. Barnes asked again.

"Whoever wrote that note, I guess."

"And who do you think that might be?"

"I have an idea, but I'd be killed for telling."

"Who would kill you?" Mr. Barnes asked.

"Certain persons," Joshua volunteered reluctantly.

"Your class has a reputation for being one of the nicest in the school, hardworking and easy to handle. The teachers have always been very fond of them, so I'm surprised at this."

"I wish I could tell you what I think," Joshua said to Mr. Barnes. "But I can't."

"I want you to go home and really think about what you know and whether you shouldn't tell me the truth," Mr. Barnes said.

"Can I go home now?"

"I thought you had a dentist's appointment."

"Right."

"*Do* you have a dentist's appointment?"

"No," Joshua said. "But I wasn't lying to you. I was lying to someone else. I told someone else I had a dentist's appointment so I wouldn't have to do something."

"I don't understand, Joshua," Mr. Barnes said, getting up

from his chair. "But in any case I want to see you in my office at eight thirty tomorrow morning with some explanation."

"Okay," Joshua said, getting up quickly.

"And don't make an appointment with the dentist for tomorrow morning."

"Okay," Joshua said. He ran down the corridor and down the steps, past Tommy Wilhelm, who shouted, "So what's up? Any problem?"

"No problem," Joshua called back. And he met up with Andrew Porter at the flagpole.

"Let's bolt," he said.

They crossed Thirty-fourth Street.

"So?" Andrew asked.

"Someone wrote a letter to Mr. Barnes saying I took the lunchbox."

"Guess who?" Andrew said, pulling his wool cap over his ears.

"Sure, but who can prove it?" Joshua said.

"You could tell Mr. Barnes about the NOs. Joey Taggart and Peter Sears and Sammy Fox might tell what happened to them."

"Are you crazy?" Joshua said.

"So what are you going to do?" Andrew reached into his pocket and gave Joshua a Kudos.

"Move to Africa," Joshua said. "I'm planning to leave tomorrow morning by boat."

They crossed Newark and headed up the hill toward Peoples Drugs.

"I mean really," Andrew said.

"I don't know," Joshua said. "I can't tell on them. And that's that."

Tommy Wilhelm followed Andrew and Joshua to Peoples Drugs. When Joshua spotted him, he was standing at the checkout counter with a Mars bar and a Milky Way, and Billy Nickel was beside him. W.V. was looking at car magazines and Jell-O was behind Tommy in line with a bag of Fritos and a liter bottle of Coca-Cola.

"Don't talk to them," Joshua said.

"Fine with me," Andrew agreed. He followed Joshua to the candy aisle.

"What if they talk to you first?" Andrew asked.

"I'll tell them to blow town," Joshua said. "What else?"

But he didn't tell them anything of the kind.

"So what's up?" Tommy Wilhelm asked when he had bought his candy. "Did Mr. Barnes give you a hard time?"

"Not at all," Joshua said.

"Just wanted to know how you were enjoying fifth grade. Right?" Tommy asked. Jell-O Hayes and W.V. laughed.

"Exactly," Joshua said.

"Hey, Joshua, I thought you had a dentist's appointment," Billy Nickel said.

"I do."

"Then why are you buying candy?" Jell-O asked.

"I bet you made it up about the dentist," W.V. said. "You're just chicken to go to Tommy's house."

"Right," Joshua said. "Scared to death." He paid for two Milky Ways.

"Hey, Josh, how's your new girlfriend?" W.V. cooed sweetly.

"Yeah," Jell-O joined in, "when are you and Sean getting *married*?"

"C'mon," Joshua said to Andrew. "Let's get out of here."

"What are you going to do?" Andrew asked, obviously afraid. "Let's go to my house. You can spend the night."

"I told you, dumbbell," Joshua said. "I'm going to Africa first thing in the morning."

At Veazy Street, Andrew turned right and Joshua ran all the way to Lowell Street and home, just in case someone was following.

chapter eight

SOMETHING WAS the matter at home. The moment Joshua walked through the front door, hung his book bag on the hook in the hall, and called out "I'm home" to the eerie silence, he knew that something was different.

"Anybody here?" he shouted. There was no answer. In the kitchen Marmalade slept on top of the apples in the fruit bowl sitting in the sun, and Plutarch was lying underneath the kitchen table licking the inside of a yogurt carton. The morning paper, which his mother never read until late afternoon when she started dinner, was opened on the counter, and the table was still gooey with the remains of Georgie's banana and yogurt. They must have left in a hurry if his mother didn't even take the time to wipe the kitchen table. There was no note and no sign of Amanda either. The clock over the stove said three fifty and Amanda was always home by three.

Upstairs, Amanda's book bag was lying on the floor of her room, her French book open on her desk to lesson ten, her basketball shorts and shirt piled in the middle of the floor. The tape recorder was playing the last song on the tape of *Les Misérables,* so there must have been an emergency, because Amanda never did anything careless like leaving the tape recorder on.

Joshua was worried. Once he'd had a nightmare about coming home to a blue house on Lowell Street, which looked in his dream exactly like his house—even Amanda's blue Schwinn was parked by the dogwood tree in the front yard. "Mom, I'm home," he had called, and the front door opened. There was another woman, not his mother, who answered the door. His mother had disappeared.

He picked up Marmalade and went, full of dread, into the living room. Maybe, he thought, something awful had happened and they had disappeared. He called his father, but Mr. Bates was out of the office. Then Joshua called Mrs. Peachtree next door, who did not know anything at all because she had just returned from Richmond, where she'd been visiting her daughter. Then he called the Franks in the house on the other side and Mrs. Frank, frantic with twins, was in her usual bad mood and said she knew nothing about any of the Bateses except that Marmalade had brought a half-dead mouse into their living room that morning and the twins had chickenpox. "Tell your mother about the cat," she said, and hung up. He got two chocolate chip cookies and sat down at the kitchen table. At four the telephone rang and it was his mother calling from Georgetown University Hospital to say that the red-haired midget had had an accident.

"What happened?" Joshua asked. He could hear strange noises in the background. Hospital noises. It made Joshua feel queasy.

"I'm not exactly sure, Joshua. Apparently he was on the roof at school and slipped. They tried to reach his father, and when they couldn't, they called me."

"Why?"

"I'm room mother for your class, Joshua."

"Oh, yeah."

"Anyway, he's fine, darling. We should be home soon. Oh, and I'm bringing Sean with us."

Joshua hung up the telephone. He lay down on the couch in the living room with Marmalade on his stomach and put a pillow over his face. Ever since Sean O'Malley arrived at Mirch Elementary School, which seemed like ten years ago, things had been going badly.

When Mrs. Bates finally came in the front door with Amanda and Georgie, Sean O'Malley wasn't with them.

"Joshua, I'd like you to come to the kitchen while I make dinner," Mrs. Bates said with an edge to her voice.

"Where's Sean?" Joshua asked.

"That's what I want to talk to you about," Mrs. Bates said.

Joshua lifted Marmalade off his stomach, put the pillow back on the couch, and followed his mother to the kitchen.

"Sean didn't come," Mrs. Bates said.

"So I see." Joshua slid into a kitchen chair and took two more chocolate chip cookies out of the jar. "How come?"

"He said he didn't want to come," Mrs. Bates said. "He asked me to drop him at his apartment, which I did."

"He had a terrible day at school," Joshua said. "Maybe that's why."

Mrs. Bates put a pot of water on the stove for pasta. "He said all the kids hate him, including you."

"Well, he's wrong."

"Things of his were stolen, he said. He was tripped. Someone's lunch was deliberately spilled on his head."

"I know, Mom. But I didn't do any of those things."

Mrs. Bates gave Joshua an odd, questioning look. "Are you sure?"

"Of course I'm sure."

"Joshua, Mr. Barnes received a letter saying that you had been very unkind to Sean."

"How do you know?" Joshua's heart was beating fast.

"Sean told me."

"Sean?" Joshua said. "How does he know?"

"Someone told him. He wouldn't say who it was."

"Brother," Joshua said, suddenly feeling very sick. "I know

about the note. Mr. Barnes called me into his office."

"What did he say to you?" Mrs. Bates sat down next to Joshua and put her hand on his arm.

"He told me to see him tomorrow morning and tell him everything I know." Joshua's voice was shaking.

"And do you know something about all this, darling?" Mrs. Bates asked.

"I don't know something," Joshua said. "I think something."

"But you are not involved in what's been happening, is that right?" his mother asked.

"That's right," Joshua said. "I promise."

Mrs. Bates kissed Joshua on the top of his head, stood up, and got the pasta from a pantry shelf. "I believe you," she said.

UPSTAIRS, Amanda was lying in the hall talking on the telephone with her bare feet on the wall.

She put her hand over the receiver.

"Tommy Wilhelm just called a second ago. He said it's an emergency."

"Thanks," Joshua said, feeling weak all over. "If he calls again, tell him I've left for Africa already."

At dinner he was too upset to eat. His father asked Amanda about her day at school, which was full of A's as usual, and he told them about the trip he'd made to New York and

77

what he had for lunch. His mother talked about Georgie's playgroup and how she'd broken a bottle of pickles at the supermarket. Amanda said she had been invited to Florida with her boyfriend's family for spring vacation and Mr. Bates said she couldn't go, so Amanda angrily excused herself to go to her room. Georgie spilled her pasta and Marmalade brought in a mouse from the garden. Finally, just as dinner was almost over, Joshua's mother brought up Sean O'Malley and the note to Mr. Barnes.

"Joshua, I want you to tell us what is going on," Mr. Bates said.

"I don't know what's going on. I can only guess."

"Are you involved?" his father asked.

"No," Joshua answered, always a little nervous with his father.

"Do you know the people who are?" Mrs. Bates asked.

"I know some of the kids involved," Joshua said. "Two for sure."

"Who are they?" his father asked.

"I can't tell."

"Why, Joshua?" Mr. Bates asked.

"I just can't."

"Why?" his father insisted.

"I don't like it when you act like a lawyer instead of my father."

"I'm sorry, Joshua," Mr. Bates said. "I didn't mean to. I only want to help."

Actually Joshua was glad to finally be talking to his parents about the NOs, even though he did not intend to tell on Tommy Wilhelm.

"Are you afraid that if you do tell us, these boys will do something to you?" his mother asked.

"Maybe." Joshua was pleased that they seemed to understand. "Everyone's afraid. Everyone in class. The boys, that is."

"Everyone?"

"A lot of people."

"Do you think a group of boys in the fifth grade are being cruel to Sean?" Mr. Bates asked.

"Yes," Joshua said.

"Why Sean?"

"Because he's new and little and wants to fit in."

"I'm not sure I understand," Mr. Bates said.

"It's just like when I flunked third grade."

"But you didn't let them hurt you," his father said.

"I guess." Joshua shrugged.

"And you got yourself promoted into the fourth grade, didn't you?" Mrs. Bates said.

"Yes," Joshua said.

"Because you took charge," Mr. Bates said.

Joshua nodded.

"Well, what I think you should do, Josh, is take charge again."

Upstairs, Joshua sat at his desk with math assignments in fractions and a composition in language arts, but he couldn't concentrate on homework. He packed his book bag with his unfinished assignments, brushed his teeth, patted the bottom bunk of his bed for Plutarch to jump up, turned off the light, and climbed into bed. He didn't fall asleep for a very long time, not until after Georgie had stopped talking to her stuffed animals and Amanda had finished with the telephone for the night and was playing her tapes, not even after his parents had come upstairs to bed. When he finally did fall asleep, he had a terrible nightmare in which he was chased and chased and chased and woke up tangled in his sheets.

chapter nine

THE NEXT MORNING Amanda called from her bedroom to say that Tommy Wilhelm was on the telephone. Joshua was awake. He was awake because he hadn't been able to get back to sleep at all since the nightmare that had woken him up in the middle of the night. And the last thing in the world he wanted to do was talk to Tommy Wilhelm. But he did.

"We're meeting by the shed at eight forty-five this morning," Tommy said. "Meet us there. It's really important."

"If I can," Joshua said. "I didn't get my math and English done last night."

"Big deal. I never do my math," Tommy said. "Did you hear about Sean falling off the roof trying to get his lunchbox?"

"I heard," Joshua said. He hadn't been able to think about

what he was going to do this morning, but he knew he had to do something.

Either he had to take charge and tell Mr. Barnes the truth, or else not. He wasn't at all sure which.

"Listen, Bates," Tommy Wilhelm said, "just be there."

"Okay," Joshua said.

But he knew very well he was not going to meet Tommy Wilhelm and the NOs at the shed. He was certain that they had something in mind. And it was not going to be very pleasant.

"I didn't know you and Tommy Wilhelm were good friends," Amanda said, examining herself in the full-length mirror in her new short-short skirt and FOREVER YOURS T-shirt.

"We're not," Joshua said.

"Well, he certainly calls a lot for an acquaintance."

"We're enemies," Joshua said irritably. "I'd like to put him out with the trash."

He started into his bedroom to get dressed.

"What do you think of this outfit?" Amanda asked. "Do you like the skirt?"

"The skirt's great," Joshua said.

"I mean look at it, Joshua. It's a new skirt."

Joshua looked.

"You look like you always do. I can't tell the difference."

"Creep," Amanda said, and slammed her bedroom door.

JOSHUA LEFT for school just after eight—and before his mother and father came downstairs with more advice about taking charge. They had no idea what a terrible day this might be for him.

At the corner of Veazy he sat on the front steps of the house where he usually waited for Andrew.

"So I guess you heard what happened to Sean yesterday," Joshua said.

"Your mother called my mother to tell her about it," Andrew said. "She said that something awful is going on and asked if I knew anything about it."

"What did your mother say?"

"She said she didn't think so but she'd ask."

"And did you tell?"

"I told about what happened to Sean all day yesterday and about the note Mr. Barnes has that blames you," Andrew said. "But I'd be crazy to tell about the NOs."

They walked along shoulder to shoulder, past Veazy and up Thirty-fourth Street.

"What do you think would happen if we did tell about the NOs?" Joshua said finally.

"They'd kill us," Andrew said.

"Tommy called this morning," Joshua said. "I think they have plans for me today."

"Are you sure?"

"He asked me to meet him at the shed at eight forty-five."

"So?"

"So I'm not going to do it," Joshua said. "But I've got to have something to say to Mr. Barnes in the next fifteen minutes."

"Are you still afraid of Tommy? Even after you fought him last year and won?" Andrew asked.

"Are you?"

"Of course I am," Andrew said. "You know me. I'm a wimp. That's why I stay clear of him."

Joshua laughed. "I'm not exactly afraid of Tommy," Joshua said. "What I *am* afraid of, though, is the power he has over the other guys. It's having the whole class turn against you that's scary."

"I know," Andrew agreed. "So what are you going to tell Mr. Barnes?"

"I don't know yet," Joshua said.

"Are you too chicken to tell him about the NOs?" Andrew said.

"Probably," Joshua said.

"Probably?" Andrew was right.

"Absolutely."

They were crossing Albermarle when they saw Sean O'Malley walking up the hill. Joshua waved. Sean did not wave back. He crossed over Albermarle and turned down

Thirty-fifth Street so he wouldn't have to meet up with Andrew and Joshua.

"What's up?" Andrew asked. "I thought you were his best friend in the world."

"Not anymore," Joshua said. "Not since he told my mother about that letter to Mr. Barnes."

They walked across Thirty-fourth Street and into the yard of Mirch Elementary just as Sean was crossing by the flagpole and going around to the back of the school.

"He's probably been asked to meet the NOs at the shed, too," Joshua said.

"Let's check."

"I don't want to check," Joshua said. "Tommy will see me, and I told him I wasn't going to come to school until I finished my homework."

"We'll check from the library window."

"I don't want Mr. Barnes to see me, either." Joshua wasn't the kind of boy to panic, but he was beginning to feel funny inside. He had to do something, and fast. "I know. I'll send Mr. Barnes a note telling him I'm sick with something contagious." But for the time being, until the bell rang for the beginning of school, he was going to go to the boys' room and hide. Unless, of course, Tommy Wilhelm arrived. And then what?

He couldn't decide what to do.

"We'll go up the back steps and look out the window on that side of the building," Andrew said.

From the window they could see the shed. W.V. and Jell-O sat on the roof. They could also see Sean O'Malley walking across the playground with Billy Nickel and Tommy Wilhelm.

"Brother," Joshua said. "It looks like the beginning of another wonderful day."

chapter ten

SEAN O'MALLEY was not in homeroom.

"Does anyone know if Sean is all right?" Mrs. Wooden asked.

No one answered. Joshua and Andrew had seen Sean twice that morning already, but they didn't raise their hands. Tommy and Billy Nickel had walked across the playground with him, and certainly some of the other fifth graders had seen him then, but no one spoke.

"Yesterday, as some of you know, Sean fell off the roof trying to get his lunchbox, which someone had put there as a joke," Mrs. Wooden said. "Is there anyone who might know how that lunchbox got there? Joshua, you were with him most of the day. Do you know anything?"

"No," Joshua said. "I mean, not really."

Mary Sellers raised her hand.

"I thought I saw him on the playground," she said.

"Did anyone else see him?" Mrs. Wooden asked.

There was no answer.

"Well, maybe it wasn't him," Mary Sellers said quietly. "Maybe it was another red-haired boy."

Sean wasn't in math class either.

Joshua passed a note to Tommy Wilhelm: WHAT DID YOU DO TO SEAN?

BEATS ME, Tommy wrote back. The note was signed NOS FOREVER.

Halfway through math class Mr. Barnes came into the room and told Joshua Bates to please come to his office.

"Best of luck," Tommy whispered as Joshua left. "I hope you're not going to be suspended."

"Who cares?" Joshua said. "I'm moving to Africa tomorrow."

He followed Mr. Barnes down the corridor to his office. Mr. Barnes told him to sit down, then closed the door. Joshua's heart was beating like a hammer on a drum.

Joshua had never seen Mr. Barnes look so grim.

"Sean O'Malley has disappeared," Mr. Barnes said.

"I guess he is absent," Joshua suggested.

"He's not absent!" Mr. Barnes snapped. "He has disappeared."

"Oh," Joshua mumbled. His throat was so dry he could hardly swallow.

"Joshua, I'm asking you again what is going on with Sean

O'Malley. We're trying to get in touch with his father, to see if he drove Sean to school this morning. But you were with him all day yesterday, and I expect you may have some idea what might have happened to Sean."

Joshua knew he was going to have to say something.

"Well, Joshua," Mr. Barnes said in a pressing tone. "What can you tell me?"

"I know," he said in a low voice.

"You know?"

"I saw him," Joshua said.

"Where?"

"I saw him walking to school up Albermarle and then later walking across the playground."

"Was he alone?" Mr. Barnes asked.

Joshua hesitated. "Yes," he said finally. "He was alone."

"And that's all you know?"

"Yes."

"You have no idea what is going on. Is that correct?"

"Yes," Joshua said.

Mr. Barnes stood up from his desk and opened the door to his office for Joshua to leave.

"I want you to know, Joshua, that I don't believe you," he said quietly.

Joshua didn't know what to say. Of course Mr. Barnes didn't believe him. He wasn't telling the whole truth. He walked out the door, past the nurse's office, the third-grade classrooms, the library, and back to math class.

While Miss Lacey was putting the homework on the board, Tommy Wilhelm passed another note.

I HOPE YOU'RE SMARTER THAN YOU USED TO BE WHEN YOU FLUNKED THIRD GRADE AND KNOW WHEN TO SHUT UP, the note said.

"Don't worry," Joshua said when the bell for next period rang. "I'm smart enough to make my own decisions."

Mr. Barnes came into Mr. Webb's class at the start of art with an announcement that the fifth and sixth grades were to meet in the auditorium for a special assembly. His voice was very grim.

Joshua looked around the classroom. Tommy Wilhelm seemed to be working hard on his bird feeder, his head down. Billy Nickel whispered something in Tommy's ear, but he didn't look up. Andrew Porter gave Joshua a look that said trouble, and Jell-O Hayes kept trying to get Tommy's attention.

Joshua took out a piece of paper and pretended to rework his design, but actually he was thinking what in the world he was going to do. He could feel the tension in the class. Everyone knew that something was wrong and probably most everyone—at least all of the boys—knew the NOs were up to no good.

Maybe, Joshua was thinking, he could pretend to be sick. Then he'd go to the nurse and the nurse would call his mother. But Mr. Barnes would probably guess that he was not actually sick. Perhaps he should tell. Go to Mr. Barnes and say that he was very sorry not to have mentioned it earlier, but there was a group in the fifth grade called the NOs, which stood for Nerds Out, and they had been responsible for the persecution of other boys and might very well be responsible for the disappearance of Sean O'Malley. Just the thought of it made Joshua feel sick. Taking charge was very difficult.

He was about to raise his hand to ask to be excused for the boys' room when Tommy Wilhelm raised his hand and told Mr. Webb that he felt sick and needed to be excused.

"Me too," Joshua said.

"You're sick too?" Mr. Webb asked, disbelieving.

"Not exactly."

Mr. Webb frowned. "What do you mean 'not exactly'?"

"I mean 'no,' " Joshua said.

"I thought so."

"But I do have to go to the bathroom," Joshua said.

"Later," Mr. Webb said. "After the meeting."

When the bell rang for the special assembly, Joshua ran out of art class to the boys' room without waiting for Andrew. Just as he passed the library, Tommy Wilhelm, who was standing by his locker, stopped him.

"If you say anything," Tommy said, his voice cocky, "you'll be sorry."

By the time Joshua got to the boys' room a group of fifth

graders were huddled in a corner discussing the special assembly.

"It's about the new kid," Adam Speth said. "Someone said he was here this morning and now he's gone."

A couple of boys waved when he walked in, but Joshua didn't wave back. He found an empty stall, closed the door, sat down, and tried to think. What would Tommy really do if he did tell? Joshua wondered. He wouldn't actually *kill* him, of course. But he might come close. He had a lot of friends to help, like Billy and W.V., and who knew who else? It wasn't like in third grade, Joshua realized. Somehow this was more serious.

He heard the bathroom door swing open and recognized the voice of Billy Nickel.

"Hello, girls," Billy said cheerfully. The boys muttered some hellos. Joshua peeked through a crack in the door of the stall. Billy was at the mirror, combing his hair so it stood up in a peak on his broad forehead. He slipped his comb into his back pocket.

Billy stood with his hands on his hips. He looked from one boy to another. "I hope all of you are smart enough to know when to keep your mouths shut?" The boys shrugged and nodded. "Good," Billy said. "Because nobody likes a nerd. Especially a red-haired midget nerd from New Jersey."

"I don't know, Billy," one of the boys said, "the new kid doesn't seem that bad." It was Jim Gray.

"Not that bad!" Billy spun and shot a hard look at Jim

Gray. "He's the worst nerd ever. And if you don't think so," warned Billy, "then maybe you'll end up getting the same treatment."

The boys mumbled in nervous agreement. Billy smiled. "And remember, nobody knows anything about what happened to the new kid. Right?"

"Right, Billy."

"Sure."

"Absolutely."

Joshua waited until he was certain all the boys had left, then stood up and swung open the stall door. Someone was staring back at him from the mirror. Joshua sighed.

He didn't recognize his own face.

Tommy was outside the boys' bathroom leaning against the cement wall with a lollipop in his mouth.

"So what do you think the assembly is about, Joshua?"

"What do you think?" Joshua said sarcastically. "The Fourth of July?"

Tommy shrugged.

"Where is he?" Joshua asked.

"Eaten by bears," Tommy said. "Where do you think?"

"I think he's in the shed tied up," Joshua said.

"You're a smart kid, Bates, if you shut up."

Joshua folded his arms across his chest.

"Are you going to tell?" Tommy asked.

"I didn't say what I was going to do."

"Tell and you're chicken stew," Tommy said, and there was a strange expression on his face.

ANDREW CAUGHT UP with Joshua outside the auditorium.

"What did Mr. Barnes want?" Andrew asked.

"He wanted to know what I knew about Sean."

Even Andrew seemed nervous. "And?"

"And I told him I saw him twice this morning but haven't seen him since."

"Which is the truth, right?"

Joshua wasn't exactly sure if it was the truth or not. Andrew was troubled.

"What do you think happened to him?" he asked Joshua.

"I think he's locked in the shed."

Andrew seemed surprised. "You know that for sure?"

"I have a feeling," Joshua said. They walked on in silence.

When Joshua and Andrew filed into the auditorium, Tommy Wilhelm, Billy Nickel, and a few other boys were already sitting in the bleachers, talking and joking in the back rows. Joshua walked to the front and sat down. The door near the front of the room suddenly swung open and Mr. Barnes walked in. He crossed the stage and stopped at the podium. He looked very unpleasant. Even from this far away, Joshua had a hard time looking Mr. Barnes in the eye. Joshua stared at his shoes instead. Mr. Barnes grabbed the edge of the podium with both hands and stared out over the room. A few kids coughed. One kid even giggled.

"On Monday of this week," Mr. Barnes said, "a new boy from New Jersey joined the fifth grade. His name is Sean O'Malley." He looked around the room and, spotting Joshua, nodded. Joshua felt sick to his stomach.

"On Tuesday some extremely unpleasant things began happening to Sean. Malicious and cruel things." He stopped and folded his arms across his chest. "And I'm sorry to say that not one of his fellow students even bothered to help or to stop these things from happening. But what is much more serious at the moment is that Sean is missing."

Joshua sneaked a sidelong look. Most of the kids had their heads lowered. We all look guilty, Joshua thought.

"We know from his father that Sean left for school this morning. In fact, some students even admit to having seen him on the playground."

Mr. Barnes inhaled deeply, as if to control his anger. He looked coldly at the kids on the bleachers.

"I want to know where Sean is."

There was whispering back and forth. But no one raised a hand, and the whispering died out.

"We're not leaving this room until I get an answer," Mr. Barnes warned. "No one knows anything?" he asked, surveying the room. His eyes swept back and forth, until they settled on Joshua T. Bates.

"Joshua," Mr. Barnes said, his voice less angry now than

disappointed. "Isn't there something, anything, you'd like to say?"

And Joshua knew just then what he had to do. Not for Mr. Barnes. Not for Andrew or Jim Gray or any of the other kids. Not even for Sean. But for Joshua T. Bates.

Joshua stood up in front of the entire assembly.

"I know what happened."

"Then come with me to my office," Mr. Barnes said.

"No," Joshua said. "I'll go get Sean and bring him back." And he stepped over Andrew and walked up the aisle of the auditorium, past Tommy Wilhelm and Billy Nickel and W.V., although he did not look at them. He didn't stop at his locker but went down the steps by the library, out the back door into the gray cold of the winter morning, across the asphalt of the playground, the frozen grass of the baseball field, to the shed at the back of the property of Mirch Elementary School. His breath was thin. The shed door was held fast with a stick through the bolt. He pulled out the stick, opened the door, and as his eyes adjusted to the darkness inside the shed he saw Sean O'Malley, just as he expected, over in the corner next to the basketballs and baseball bats and bases, his eyes covered with a bandanna, his mouth stuffed with a handkerchief, his outstretched legs tied at the ankles, his hands tied behind his back. First he untied the bandanna and took the old handkerchief out of Sean's mouth. But Sean didn't talk.

Joshua didn't know what to say.

He untied the slender rope securing Sean's hands behind his back. When they were free, Sean rubbed his wrists, reached in his pocket, and took out his mittens.

"You must be freezing," Joshua said, untying the rope at Sean's ankles. "I know you're really mad at me. My mother said you were. And I know you think I've been involved with Tommy Wilhelm."

Sean didn't reply but kept his eyes on Joshua, watching him untie the rope.

"Mr. Barnes called a special assembly," Joshua said. "He knows you're missing. Your father said you came to school, and some people, like me, saw you this morning." He stood up. "There," he said. "You're untied now."

Slowly Sean got to his feet. He picked up his lunchbox, which was sitting in the middle of the sports equipment, put on his cap, and rubbed his runny nose with the back of his mitten.

"He asked did anyone know where you were," Joshua said. "So I said I did. I guessed in the first place and then Tommy Wilhelm admitted that you were in the shed." He walked out of the shed, keeping pace with Sean, who walked fast, facing straight ahead. "I told Mr. Barnes I would go get you," Joshua said, following Sean up the back steps into the school.

For a moment Joshua thought that Sean was going to bolt, but he didn't. He walked right beside Joshua, down the corridor, past the fifth- and sixth-grade classrooms, past the administration offices, down the steps, and through the double doors into the auditorium.

A great hush fell over the room as Sean O'Malley, followed by Joshua right behind, walked past the rows of students to the stage, and up the steps to Mr. Barnes, who hugged Sean, lifting him off his feet.

"There is an organization in the fifth grade called the NOs, which means Nerds Out," Joshua began quietly, his voice shaking as he spoke. "The head of the group is Tommy Wilhelm, and a lot of the boys in the fifth grade belong. They persecute kids they don't like, and that's what's been happening to Sean O'Malley."

"How long have you known about this group?" Mr. Barnes asked.

"For quite a long time," Joshua said.

"Why didn't you let me know?" Mr. Barnes said.

"I was afraid," Joshua said.

"And what did they do to you?" Mr. Barnes asked Sean.

"They tied me up in the shed," Sean said, too quietly for anyone but Joshua and Mr. Barnes to hear.

"Tommy Wilhelm?" Mr. Barnes said. "Will you stand up?"

No one turned around to look, but out of the corner of his eye Joshua could see Tommy Wilhelm stand up very slowly in the back of the auditorium. "I will meet you in my office, Tommy," Mr. Barnes said. "And I strongly suggest that anyone who has had anything to do with this march himself to my office immediately. Don't think you can hide. I assure you I will find out who you are."

JOSHUA WAS HARDLY aware of what came next. It had all happened so quickly. He didn't even know how he felt exactly. All he knew was it was over.

After Mr. Barnes dismissed the assembly and ordered everyone back to class, and when the groans died down, Joshua followed Mr. Barnes and Sean up the aisle toward the auditorium exit. Suddenly Joshua became aware of a strange commotion—first from one side of the room, and then from the other, then from all sides of the room, front and back. Kids were clapping, and smiling, and yelling "Way to go!" and "All right!"

Even Mr. Barnes and Sean were clapping.

Joshua couldn't believe it. They were clapping for him!

JOSHUA WALKED HOME ALONE. Andrew had flute practice, so Joshua took his books for homework, his heavy jacket, and his cap and walked home through a light snow, feeling wonderful for the first time in a very long time.

Inside the blue house on Lowell Street there was a note from his mother saying that she had gone to the market with Georgie, that Amanda was at basketball practice, and that there was a snack in the fridge. He picked up Marmalade and went into the living room with the comics. He didn't even hear anyone at the front door while he was reading, but when he heard his mother's car in the driveway, he went to the door and there on the porch was a note. DEAR JOSHUA, the note said. MAYBE WHEN YOU GET TO SCHOOL TOMORROW WE CAN BE FRIENDS. SINCERELY, SEAN PATRICK O'MALLEY.

Susan Shreve is the author of many books for children, including *The Flunking of Joshua T. Bates; Joshua T. Bates in Trouble Again; The Goalie; Lucy Forever and Miss Rosetree, Shrinks* (winner of the Edgar Allan Poe Award); and *The Gift of the Girl Who Couldn't Hear*.

A graduate of the University of Pennsylvania, Ms. Shreve is a creative writing professor at George Mason University. She lives in Washington, D.C.

Joshua T. Bates in Trouble Again

by Susan Shreve

It's not easy being Joshua T. Bates! After flunking third grade and repeating a semester, Joshua has finally been promoted to fourth grade. But moving forward and fitting in are two different matters, especially with Tommy Wilhelm, Joshua's sworn enemy, leading the class. Joshua will do almost anything to prove to Tommy he's not a nerd—even if that means stealing his dad's Swiss Army knife. And that's when the *real* trouble begins.

The Flunking of Joshua T. Bates

by Susan Shreve

It's the worst possible end to a great summer vacation: Joshua Bates finds out he has to repeat the third grade. His teachers say he needs another year "to mature." What do they expect from a nine-year-old? A beard?

The first day of school is a complete nightmare. The fourth graders think he's a freak, the kids in his new class are babies, and his teacher looks like a two-ton tank. Joshua is totally miserable. Will he ever catch up—or is he stuck in the third grade forever?

"Crisply humorous."
—*The Bulletin of the Center for Children's Books*

"Touching, funny, and realistic."
—*School Library Journal*

A KNOPF PAPERBACK PUBLISHED BY ALFRED A. KNOPF, INC.